EREC AND ENID

EREC AND ENID

adapted and retold by
BARBARA SCHILLER

illustrated by ATI FORBERG

E. P. DUTTON & CO., INC. NEW YORK

Other Books by
Barbara Schiller

Audun and His Bear
The Kitchen Knight
The Vinlanders' Saga
The White Rat's Tale

Published simultaneously in Canada by Clarke,
Irwin & Company Limited, Toronto and Vancouver

SBN: 0-525-29346-9 (Trade) SBN: 0-525-29347-7 (DLLB)
Library of Congress Catalog Card Number: 70-116887

Printed in the U.S.A.
First Edition

"This adventure is about Erec of the Round Table—a story which those who earn their living by storytelling usually spoil. Now I, Chrétien de Troyes, shall begin my tale. It will be remembered as long as Christendom lasts. That is my boast. . . ."

Once upon an Easter day King Arthur held a rich and royal court in his town of Cardigan.

Many a brave and hardy knight came there with his noble lady. Of fair and gentle damsels there were a full five hundred.

When the feast was at its finish, King Arthur arose and joyful said, "Noble knights and ladies all, tomorrow we shall hunt the White Stag as our fathers did before us. And very delightful the hunt will be."

With that the king signaled the end of the meal.

Now the knights were free to please their ladies. Some told stories. Others sang and talked of love. Everyone in the great stone hall was given over to gladness except my lord Gawain.

"Sire," said he to the king, "whosoever kills the White Stag will then kiss the fairest damsel of the court."

"That is the ancient Eastertide custom," replied King Arthur to his nephew.

"I think only great ill can come of it. For here are five hundred damsels of high birth and beauty. Each of these gentle maidens has a bold and gallant knight sworn to serve her. Every knight thinks his damsel is the fairest. Of these proud knights all but one will be jealous and angered. Think you that the jealous knights will not defend their slighted damsels?"

"Be that as it may," answered Arthur, "a king's word must not be denied. Tomorrow at daybreak we shall all go gaily to hunt the White Stag in the Forest of Adventure."

And so it was that the new day dawned on a debonair company gathered in the castle forecourt. Armed with bows and arrows, dressed in short jackets and well mounted, the knights were ready for a forest ride. Off they went at the king's command, happy with morning laughter.

Now this same morning Queen Guinevere had awakened late. To make up for time thus lost she took only one attendant and rode swiftly toward the forest.

After the queen and her damsel there followed a knight of the Round Table named Erec. He was young and fair and brave. Great was his fame at court, and rightly so. For never was there a man his age of greater knighthood. All in splendid silk he came riding, golden spurs at his heels, with no weapon but a hunting bow.

When Erec came up with the queen he greeted her and said, "My lady, if it is to your pleasure I shall accompany you to the hunt."

"Fair friend," said she, "my thanks. For better company I could not have."

While they were riding at full gallop, the hunting party had sighted the White Stag. Many were the cries of "Ho" and "Halloo."

Horns were winded and arrows unleashed. The hounds plunged forward—running, attacking, baying. And before them all rode King Arthur.

But as the queen, Erec, and the damsel rode through the forest they saw no sign of the hunt. So they drew rein and listened for the sound of horn or baying of hound. Of horse, huntsman, and hound they heard nothing. Which way to ride in the Forest of Adventure?

They were debating this question when the queen saw an armed knight cantering down a woodland path. His shield of gold and blue was slung about his neck and his lance was in his hand. Beside him rode a lady of noble bearing. Before them came a crooked dwarf carrying a knotted whip.

So comely and graceful was this knight that the queen wished to know who he was.

"Lunette," said she to her damsel, "go and bid yonder fair knight and his lady to come hither."

Lunette, daughter to a count and a brunette of charm and courtesy, guided her horse toward the knight.

But her path was blocked by the dwarf, who flicked his cruel whip.

"Halt," he ordered. "You shall go no farther."

"Dwarf, let me pass. The queen sends me here to speak with your master."

"Go back. It is not proper for you to address a knight of my master's excellence."

Lunette was not accustomed to mean and ugly manners. She urged her horse forward, thinking to pass the villainous dwarf by force.

But he brought his whip back and then forward to her face. Lunette raised her arm and warded off this evil blow. The dwarf struck again, bringing the knotted whip down on her bare hand.

Poor Lunette, there was nothing else she could do now but ride back to the queen.

When Guinevere saw the gentle damsel wounded and weeping, she was sorely grieved and greatly angered.

"I must know what sort of a knight this is who allows such a monster to strike a lady."

The queen turned to Erec. "Fair friend, go to the knight and bid him come to me this instant."

Erec gave spur to his horse and galloped straight toward the armed knight.

But the dwarf rode forward and forced Erec to rein in his horse. "Stand back. You have no business here."

"Let me pass," said Erec, thrusting the dwarf to one side.

With that the villainous creature gave Erec a great blow on the face.

Even as he felt the pain of the whiplash, Erec knew he would not have the satisfaction of striking back. For a blow against the servant was a blow against the master. And of what use was his hunting bow against the lance and sword of the arrogant knight?

Back Erec rode to the queen.

"My lady," he said, "the armed knight rides off apace, and I must follow after. Whether it be near or far I shall find arms and armor and challenge him to battle. Look for me to return by the third day, but whether sad or joyous I know not."

Guinevere wished Erec godspeed and looked after him until he was to be seen no more.

Then through the woods she heard the horn's high notes sounding the kill. She and her damsel followed the call and came upon the hunting party, who were in great good humor. For Arthur had outstripped all others and slain the stag.

Thus it was that the king rode back to Cardigan with his queen by his side and the White Stag borne before him as was right and fitting.

But when supper was done, and the king said he would now bestow the kiss as was the custom, a great murmur arose. Each knight vowed that his damsel was the fairest in the hall; each swore to prove his gallant claim with lance or sword.

Then Gawain drew the king to one side and said, "Sire, do not award the Kiss of the White Stag."

"I must, for I have given my word to observe this ancient Eastertide custom."

"Delay then, sire," advised Gawain.

"If it pleases you, dear lord," said Guinevere, "wait until the third day when Erec will return."

"Gentle lady, that pleases me well," replied the king. "We shall do as you suggest."

15

Now all this while Erec had been steadily following the knight, but at a distance. When they came to a fine town, strong and well placed, Erec gave his horse its head.

Straight through the gate went the armed knight, the damsel, and the crooked dwarf. And following close after came Erec.

Within the town there was a great joy of fair knights and ladies. Some played at dicing, backgammon, and the pleasant

game of love. Others fed their sparrow hawks and aired their falcons. Then the knight, the damsel, and the dwarf came riding in and all pastimes stopped.

Three by three the knights and ladies stepped forth. They greeted the armed knight with great courtesy and also his courtly damsel. But none took note of Erec, for no one knew him. Thus it was that Erec was able to follow close upon the knight as he made his way through the thronged streets. After Erec saw him enter his lodgings, he rode on in high spirits.

He passed a manor house, small and not in the best repair,

and there he halted. For seated before the main door was a comely gentleman with white hair. His jacket and hose were shabby but his face and bearing were courteous, pleasing, and frank.

Surely such a goodly man will have a night's lodging for me, thought Erec. He turned through the open gate into the yard and saluted the gentleman.

"Kind sir, could you give me a lodging place this night?"

"Be welcome, fair sir. My house shall be as your own."

Erec dismounted and walked with his host to the stable. Sir Liconal, for such was the goodly knight's name, saw to the comfort of Erec's horse and put fresh sweet hay and oats before him. Then he led his guest into the hall.

There he summoned his wife and his daughter. "They are doing I know not what it is ladies busy themselves with, but be assured they will find it very delightful to have your company in our hall."

The lady came in with her daughter. Very handsome was the mother and sweeter still was the flower born of so fair a stem. What shall one say of this maiden's beauty? Nature had used all her skill in forming Enid. Truly she was made to be looked at.

Now when Enid saw the debonair young knight, she drew back a step, for she did not know him. Erec for his part was amazed to behold such beauty. Her dress without was poor—plain white linen carefully mended—but within her form was surpassingly fair.

"Daughter dear," said the elderly knight, "take Sir Erec by the hand and show him all honor."

With courtesy Enid led Erec up the stairs and prepared a room for his comfort. She laid cushions upon the couches. She placed a fine white cloth upon a table by the fire, and spoke the while with Erec in words of charm and wit.

Then the four of them sat down to supper. Erec with his host and hostess to either side and the maiden opposite. A

manservant brought water for washing in two basins and set out bread, fruit, and wine. This man was the only servant in the household, and very skillful he was in stewing meat and preparing birds on the spit.

The supper was simple, but the birds were crisp without and tender within. The fruit was sun-ripened and the bread made by Enid's hand was of fine texture.

When the table was cleared and the ladies had retired, Erec turned to Sir Liconal.

"Fair host, there are some questions I would like to ask of you."

"And right willingly will I answer if I can."

"The first," said Erec, "concerns the town through which I passed. From whence comes the throng of chivalry that crowds every corner?"

"These are the knights and nobles of the country round about. Tomorrow is the Festival of the Sparrow Hawk, and there is no one young or old who would stay away."

Sir Liconal offered Erec a comfit from a glazed jar.

"Ah, tomorrow there will be a great stir, for the finest sparrow hawk imaginable will be placed upon a silver perch in the marketplace. Whoever wishes to gain this superb hawk must have a lady who is comely, courteous, and clever. She it is who will step forth and lift the hawk from its perch."

Erec laughed. "Surely there will be many a bold knight eager to defend the worth of his lady above all others?"

"Once that was so, but for the past two years the same knight has won the hawk without a word of opposition."

The white-haired knight ate a comfit. "Now, fair friend, what is your next question?"

"Do you know of a knight whose shield is colored gold and blue and who rides in the company of a courtly lady and a crooked dwarf?"

Surprised, Sir Liconal replied, "That is he of whom I just spoke, the Knight of the Sparrow Hawk."

Quickly Erec said, "I do not like that knight." Then more slowly he said, "May it not displease you, but tell me why a maiden of your daughter's beauty and wit wears dress and kirtle so poor and patched?"

"You may be sure it grieves me to see her so," said Sir Liconal. "But poverty has played sport with me, and war has taken my land and mortgaged my manor. Yet Enid would be dressed in cloth of gold if I gave consent to her marriage. There is not a nobleman hereabout who does not

want my daughter for his wife. But I am waiting for someone worthy of her. Neither count nor king need be ashamed to marry a maiden so wondrous fair as Enid."

Now Erec and his host rose from the table and went downstairs to the hall.

When Sir Liconal saw his wife and daughter there he smiled and turned to Erec.

"Enid is my joy and my comfort, my wealth and my treasure. With her beside me I care not a marble for all the rest of the world."

Erec gazed steadfastly at the maiden. "Fortunate indeed is the man who wins Enid for his wife."

To this Sir Liconal made no answer but spoke instead about the Knight of the Sparrow Hawk.

"On my word," said Erec, "I would happily challenge him for that hawk if I had sword and armor."

"A fine sword you shall have," said the white-haired knight. "And armor too if you will wear it."

"Right gladly," replied Erec, clasping Sir Liconal's hand.

"Wait," said his host, "a young and debonair knight might well be ashamed to wear helmet and hauberk as old-fashioned as that which I offer."

"Say no more, fair friend. I am happy to borrow that which you will lend. But now I shall ask a further boon of you. It is one for which I shall make just return if God favors me with fortune."

"Ask with confidence, for whatever I am able to give shall be yours."

Erec then said, "I wish to defend the hawk on behalf of your daughter. If I take her with me, then I will truly have good reason to claim that she is entitled to the hawk. For what damsel is even one-hundredth part as beautiful as Enid?"

"That is true," replied Sir Liconal, and nothing more said he.

"Sir," said Erec, "I would not ask you so great a boon if I were no more than a newly made knight. I am the son of the King of Outer Wales and a knight of the Round Table as well."

Taking his daughter by the hand, Sir Liconal led her to Erec. "I give you my beloved daughter."

Now there was high-spirited happiness in the hall. Enid's father was greatly delighted and her fair mother wept tears of joy. Erec had that which his heart most desired. And Enid was well pleased and happy that her betrothed was valiant and courteous, handsome and of great charm.

You may be sure that they sat up very late that night in gay and gallant conversation.

And yet so eager was Erec for battle that he was up before dawn. He heard mass and then hastened to the hall and asked for his arms.

Enid put on his armor, the hauberk and the helmet. She fastened the sword at Erec's side and ordered his horse brought to the front door.

Neither block nor stirrup needed Erec, but straight from the ground he leaped into the saddle. Now Enid gave him the shield and placed the lance in his hand.

Sir Liconal led out a horse for his daughter. It was a handsome bay, but its saddle and harness were worn and well weathered.

Enid needed no urging to mount and ride off at Erec's side. Sir Liconal and his lady watched until they could see the comely pair no more.

Now when Erec and Enid came into the town all the people great and small turned to stare.

They smiled and laughed and made such talk as this: "In truth that newly made knight is wearing his grandsire's armor" or "Surely the damsel is dressed in a gown grown old in her grandame's day."

But as Erec and Enid passed through the streets the knights and ladies looked more carefully at them.

"Yonder knight is of noble bearing. From whence does he come?" Many praised the beauty and grace of the maiden. "In truth," men said one to another, "the sparrow hawk should be hers."

While all thus stood and gazed and talked, Erec and Enid rode on unheeding and without delay to the marketplace. There they took their stand close by the sparrow hawk and awaited the arrogant knight.

Before long they saw a noisy procession coming toward the marketplace. At its head and riding proudly was the Knight of the Sparrow Hawk attended by the damsel and the dwarf.

A merry crowd of knights, squires, and damsels hurried after him. Not a one of them wanted to miss a minute of the battle. They knew it would soon be finished. Bold the challenger might be, but who could match a champion as peerless as the Knight of the Sparrow Hawk?

He for his part rode straight to where the hawk stood upon its silver perch. He said to his damsel, "My lady, take this perfect bird as your just portion, for none is so wondrous fair and full of grace as you."

"Not so," cried Erec. "There is a better damsel who claims this hawk. Much more fair is she and of greater courtesy."

The wrath of the Knight of the Sparrow Hawk at these bold words can be imagined.

But Erec gave him no heed and bid Enid step forth. "Now all people can see that I make no idle boast when I say that other maidens are to you as the pale moon is to the glowing sun. Fair lady, lift the hawk from its perch, for it is right that you should have it."

At these words the arrogant knight turned to Erec. "Who are you that dares thus challenge me?"

"I am a knight from another land."

"Madness has brought you here. You will pay dearly for the hawk."

"In what coin?" asked Erec boldly.

"Your sword or your life. I have never been beaten in battle."

"Then God help me," said Erec, "for never have I wanted to fight more than I do now."

The marketplace was cleared to make a field of battle. Erec

and the knight galloped to opposite sides of the place. Then they turned, spurred their horses, and drove at each other. So great was the force with which they came together that shields were pierced and lances split. Saddle bows were broken and stirrups lost.

Both men fell to the ground and their horses dashed off into the crowd. Though bruised from the lance blows, they jumped to their feet and drew their swords.

The throng that gathered closer gasped at the fierce onslaught. So great were the sword blows that first the knight's helmet and then Erec's were crushed.

They rained blows about each other's neck and shoulders. Shields were cut and hauberks shattered. No mere knight's play was this. The silver swords were crimson, and bright blood lay upon the ground.

But no man can fight so lustily for long. Now their blows became light and listless.

"Hold," cried the Knight of the Sparrow Hawk. "Our blows are so weak that they are worthless. Let us withdraw and rest awhile to regain our strength."

"Well said," replied Erec. "See how your fair damsel weeps

for you as does my gentle maid. For the sake of our ladyloves we must strive with greater strength and thus finish our fight the sooner."

And so they rested and Erec looked upon Enid. Her love and beauty inspired him with renewed boldness. Then his thoughts turned to the wrongs he and Lunette, the queen's damsel, had suffered from the villainous dwarf and his arrogant master. Anger revived his strength and he called out to the knight. "We have rested too long. Have at it again!"

Whereupon they came together with all the force and skill of expert swordsmen. The knight lunged and Erec parried. Even so his shield was cleaved through and a span cut from the side of his hauberk. Steel met flesh but the blow was a glancing one and Erec was not a whit dismayed.

He gave back better than he had received—a violent blow to the shoulder that cut through shield and hauberk and reached the bone. But the Knight of the Sparrow Hawk fought back. In truth these knights were even in honors and could not gain a foot of ground one from the other.

They were hard and dangerous fighters, battling now without protection, for their shields were hacked to pieces and their hauberks hopelessly torn.

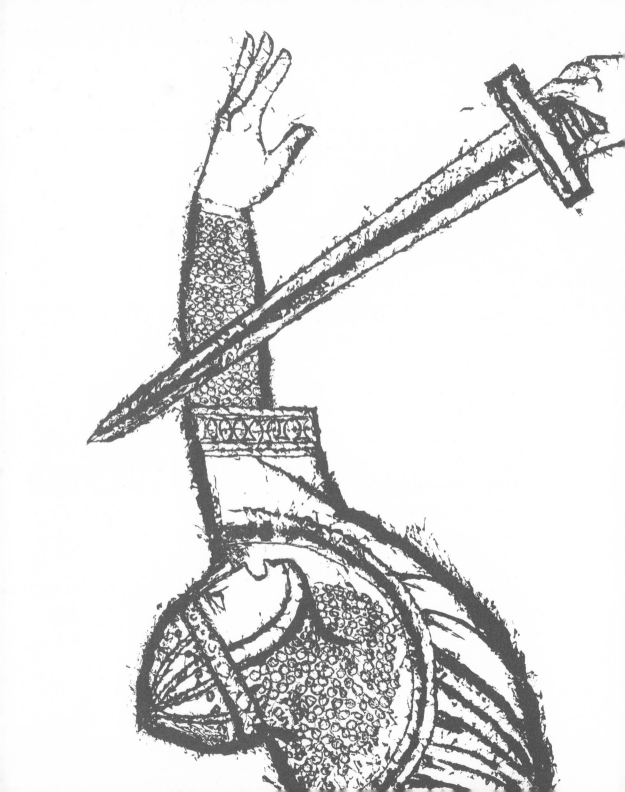

Erec smote the knight hard upon the helmet once, twice, and then a third time in quick succession. His helmet was split, his head bleeding. He stumbled and staggered and fell to the ground.

Erec dragged off his foe's helmet. He thought again of the insults done by the dwarf in the forest and was ready to slay the master.

"Mercy," cried the knight. "Killing me will bring you no further glory. Take my sword, for I am your prisoner."

When Erec hesitated the knight asked, "Why do you hate me? For I never saw you that I can remember, nor have I ever done you any wrong."

Then Erec said, "Yesterday in the Forest of Adventure you permitted your dwarf to strike first a lady and then a knight. I am that knight, Erec of the Round Table. Did you think I would let such a grave offense go unpunished?"

The vanquished knight did not reply.

Erec continued. "Go as my prisoner to Queen Guinevere at Cardigan. Surrender yourself, your damsel, and your dwarf to her to do as she will. Tell the queen that tomorrow I shall come to court bringing with me a maiden so fair and wise and fine that in the wide world she has no match. Now, sir knight, what is your name?"

"I am Sir Ider, who until this hour no man had vanquished. But now I have found a better man than I, and so right willingly do I pledge you my faith."

Erec accepted his word, and all who were present—knights and ladies, squires and damsels—witnessed the agreement. Most rejoiced for the gentle daughter of Sir Liconal, but those who were devoted to Sir Ider were downcast.

Ider did not tarry, but mounted his horse and accompanied by the damsel and the dwarf set forth straightaway through woods and plain to Cardigan.

When Ider entered the castle gate a hundred knights stood waiting, and foremost among them was Sir Gawain. He helped the lady from her horse and then turned to Ider, who had dismounted.

"Sir, the queen espied you from her bower and recognized you and your companions. Even from that distance my lady could see that you had been through great danger and she would know the outcome of the battle without delay."

Ider bowed, and accompanied by the damsel and the dwarf followed my lord Gawain into the presence of the king and the queen.

When she saw this knight, Guinevere could keep her peace no longer.

"Sir Knight, do you come as Erec's prisoner or are you here to boast of his defeat or death?"

Ider bowed low and saluted first the queen and then King
Arthur. "I come before you as the prisoner of a most noble
and valiant knight. Yesterday my dwarf lashed the face of
that knight. Today Erec overcame me at arms and defeated
me most roundly. Now I surrender myself, my damsel, and
my dwarf to you to do with as you please. Thus Erec bade me
do and right willingly have I done so."

Guinevere quickly asked, "And did Erec tell you when he
would come again to Cardigan?"

"Yes, my lady. Tomorrow he will come to this castle and
with him will be a damsel who is the fairest of all I have ever
known."

The queen, who was a lady both sensible and kind, asked the knight his name and then spoke to him courteously. "You speak with grace and courage, Sir Ider. You have thrown yourself upon my mercy and I assure you that I have no desire to seek your harm."

Guinevere arose then and said to King Arthur, "Dear lord, yesterday you listened to my suggestion to wait for Erec's return. Now I ask you to give me good counsel in the matter of this comely knight."

"Release Ider, sweet lady, and permit him to join my household and my court."

And so it was done, and with no reluctance on Ider's part, you may be sure.

Now no sooner had Ider departed from the field of battle than a jubilation arose about Erec. Great and small, thin and stout—everyone talked of his fame and praised his knighthood.

When Erec and Enid rode back to her father's house a gay procession went with them. For what knight and lady or damsel and squire would not hasten to share the happiness of Erec and Enid?

And those who were present that night witnessed a delightful scene. Erec sat down first and then the others in order of their rank seated themselves upon the couches, the cushions, and the bare benches. At Erec's side sat the radiant damsel Enid with the much-disputed sparrow hawk upon her wrist. She fed it a plover's wing. All could see how gay she was and great was the rejoicing for her happiness.

Then Erec addressed Sir Liconal and his lady wife. "Fair host, fair friend, you have done me great honor and handsomely shall it be repaid you. Tomorrow I shall take your daughter to King Arthur's court and soon thereafter you will come to witness our marriage. Afterward you will be escorted into my father's country, where two towns shall be yours. One was built in the time of Adam and a famous place it is. The other is so strong and fine that its people fear neither king nor emperor. Cloth of gold, dappled furs, and splendid silks will go with you to adorn yourself and your dear wife."

It was an agreeable evening with food and wine, song and good cheer. When it was time to separate, everyone went home as merry as when they had come.

In the morning when the dawn was bright, Erec commanded the horses to be saddled. Then he and Enid bade farewell to Sir Liconal and his lady. The good knight and his fair wife kissed them both again and again and could not keep back their tears. No more could Enid, for such is the way of love and affection between parents and children.

But once on the road to Cardigan, Enid was merry and played with her hawk, the only treasure she had ever owned. Erec rode by her side and could not look at her enough, for

44

the more he looked at Enid, the more she pleased him. He gave her a kiss and she returned it. In truth their love was a perfect match and each had stolen the other's heart away.

It was nearing noon when they came to the castle of Cardigan. They should have been glad to arrive there at the king's court, yet both would have been happy if this journey together had never come to an end.

Now as soon as Erec and Enid rode up to the entrance, the king and queen came down to greet them. Arthur was in a merry mood and caught up the damsel and lifted her down from her horse. He did Enid further honor by taking her hand and leading her up to the great stone hall. After them Erec and Guinevere went up, also hand in hand while he told her of his adventure.

Waiting in the great hall were so many knights that no one could call by name even a tenth of them.

When Enid saw all this array of knights looking steadfastly at her, she bowed her head and blushed. But embarrassment which makes most maidens graceless made Enid all the more lovely.

The king led her to a seat on his right hand and then spoke to his court.

"My lords, the time has now come to bestow the Kiss of the White Stag. Is there one amongst you who would doubt that Enid is the fairest of the fair?"

They all cried with one accord, "Bestow the kiss upon Enid."

And so it was that King Arthur in his castle of Cardigan did follow the ancient Eastertide custom of the White Stag, and never more fairly was the kiss bestowed.

"Here ends the adventure of Erec's courtship and betrothal. It is all that I, Chrétien de Troyes, am going to tell you this day about the valiant Erec and the radiant Enid."

Barbara Schiller has added a second Arthurian legend to her growing list of adapted tales for children: *The Kitchen Knight, The White Rat's Tale, The Vinlanders' Saga* and *Audun and His Bear* (one of the children's books in the American Institute of Graphic Arts exhibit for 1967–1968). Mrs. Schiller is a graduate of Syracuse University and lives in New York City with her husband and two sons.

Ati Forberg is a prominent children's book and jacket illustrator. Among her other illustrated titles are *Jeanne D'Arc* by Aileen Fisher and *A Girl and Her Room* by Phyllis McGinley. Mrs. Forberg's illustrations for *Erec and Enid* impart the dramatic character of early medieval art. Her art is reproduced in a burnt-sienna tone. Mrs. Forberg, the daughter of Bauhaus architect Walter Gropius, is also married to an architect. She lives in Brooklyn Heights, New York, with her husband and two daughters.

The display type is set in Weiss Initials and the text type is set in Granjon. The book is printed by offset.